I0546999

Brutus Finds a Collar

Dyslexic Friendly Edition

Tif E. Boots

Illustrated by Syranity Barker

DF Version ISBN-13: 978-1-963272-23-9

ShelteringTree.Earth, LLC Publishing
PO Box 973, Eagle Lake, FL 33839

ShelteringTreeMedia.com

What is a "Dyslexic Friendly" Book?

Sheltering Tree Media has taken steps to make our books more friendly for those who live with dyslexia. While the following principles will not make every book readable for every reader, it is our best effort to create products that encourage reading and to support all readers.

Throughout the book, we use a font named OpenDyslexic. This is a free font that is designed to help dyslexic readers distinguish each letter from the others. For more information about OpenDyslexic, how it differs from other fonts, and research behind the font, visit their website: www.opendyslexic.com.

In our books created for children, we use a font size which provides the reader with plenty of spacing between the letters (which is called *kerning*). The bigger, wider font tends to be easier to the reader's eyes.

The space between each word is increased (this is called *word spacing*). This helps better to distinguish when one word ends and the next begins. The line spacing is greater than most common fonts (this is called *leading*). This all should help with readability.

Whenever possible, the text is Left-Aligned but it is not justified on the right side. Allowing the right side of a paragraph to remain *rough* keeps the word spacing consistent throughout.

Our Dyslexic Friendly books are printed on cream or ivory paper which is also thicker than the average book page. This minimizes the sharp contrast of black-on-white pages as well as bleedthrough of text from the previous page.

Finally, Sheltering Tree Media has made colored overlays available when you purchase a book through our online store. You can find these overlays at ShelteringTreeMedia.com/shop/dyslexic-friendly.

These are some of the principles we use to create a book as readable as possible to those living with dyslexia. Some may find this helpful; some may not. Please provide us with any insights you might have to improve our Dyslexic Friendly principles. We pray this will enable many to heighten their love for reading.

Dedication

For My Girls.

You will forever be my inspirations.

BRUTUS FINDS A COLLAR

Under the fence that circled the pond, through the garden where the berries grow, over the green grassy hill and past the old red barn, Scrump ran. Brutus was after him!

Scrump ran around his oak tree three times, but each time, Brutus got closer. Then Scrump dived into his little rabbit hole. Brutus ran around the tree again before he noticed Scrump was gone.

"Hey, no fair," barked Brutus. "I can't fit down there."

Just then, an acorn fell from the branches high above and hit Brutus on the head. Brutus looked up just in time to move as a second acorn fell from the tree.

"You big bully," screamed a squirrel as he threw another nut. "Leave that poor bunny alone."

Scrump crawled out of his hole and sat next to Brutus. "What are you talking about?" he asked. "Brutus isn't a bully. He is my friend. We were just playing."

The squirrel stopped throwing nuts and looked down at Scrump. "Are you sure?" the squirrel asked. "He looked so mean chasing you."

"Yes, I'm sure," said Scrump.

"You should make sure you know what's going on before you start fighting," said Brutus.

"I'm...uh...I mean, I'm sorry. I hope I didn't hurt you," the squirrel stammered. "I guess now you won't want to play with me."

"You didn't hurt me," said Brutus. "I'll still play."

"Yeah," said Scrump. "Tag is more fun with three playing."

"I'm Charlie," said the squirrel as he climbed down the tree.

"I'm Brutus and this is Scrump." said Brutus. "Scrump is it!" He tapped Scrump's ear and ran.

Charlie ran away from Scrump, too, and Scrump chased after them.

They ran past the old red barn, over the grassy hill, and to the garden.

Scrump caught up to Brutus and tagged him.

Brutus caught up to Charlie and tagged him.

Charlie saw a cherry tree ahead of them near the garden and ran to climb it. When his friends ran by, he could jump down on them.

Brutus passed the cherry tree first then stopped suddenly.

Scrump had looked over his shoulder to look for Charlie and nearly ran into Brutus. "Why did you stop? Scrump asked. "Charlie's going to catch us."

"I see something," he told Scrump as Charlie jumped down from the tree.

"What is it?" Charlie asked.

"I don't know. It is shiny, though." said Brutus.

Charlie crept forward with his belly low to the ground and his tail fluffed up and pointed forward over the top of his head.

Brutus lowered his head and the fur between his shoulders stood up as he stepped closer to the shining object.

Scrump was not nearly as brave as his friends. He sat up on his hind legs, his ears perked up and twitching but he was not able to move any closer.

"Hey, I have one of those," said Brutus. "It's called a collar, but mine is thick and leather. This one is much smaller."

"I've seen yours," said Scrump when he was able to move again. "It suits you, but who would this one suit? It looks dainty compared to yours."

"Let's find out who it belongs to and return it," suggested Charlie.

Brutus picked up the collar, and the three friends walked back to the barn. There they found a tiny field mouse.

"Do you know who lost this, Mr. Mouse?" Scrump asked.

"No, I don't," squeaked the mouse. "Try down by the pond."

"OK, thank you," said Brutus. And they walked to the pond.

By the edge of the pond, they saw a frog sitting on a lily pad. "Excuse us, Mr. Frog, do you know whose this is?" Brutus asked, mumbling around the collar in his teeth.

The frog blinked giant orange eyes and said, "Riiibet."

"Is that frog for yes, or *no*?" Charlie whispered to Scrump.

The frog blinked again and said, "Riiibet."

"Well, that's not much help," said Scrump. "Let's try by the woods behind the barn."

The friends thanked the frog and raced to the edge of the woods. Brutus was good at running but Scrump was able to zip back and forth in front of him. Charlie was not as fast as them in the tall grass between the pond and the woods, but once they got close to the tree line, he was able to climb a tree and jump from branch to branch.

Soon they came upon a snake sunning herself on a rock.

"Excuse us," mumbled Brutus around the collar clenched between his teeth.

"We are looking for whoever lost this," Scrump explained, pointing to the collar.

"Oh," replied the snake. "That's mine," she hissed.

Brutus, Scrump and Charlie looked at each other uncertainly.

"How can it be yours?" asked Brutus. "It looks like it would be too big."

"Yeah," agreed Scrump. "And you have no shoulders to help keep it in place."

"Wouldn't you just slither right out of it?" asked Charlie.

"Oh, fine," hissed the snake. "You caught me. It's not mine."

"Why would you lie?" asked Scrump.

"I think it would help me," the snake said. "When I move around in my nest, my eggs roll around. I thought I could put it around them, and they would stop moving."

"Even if you want it, it's not right to lie and claim something is yours." Charlie scolded the snake.

"I know," said the snake. "I'm sorry, I just don't know what to do about my eggs. It's not safe for them to roll around so much."

"I have an idea," exclaimed Brutus. "Will you wait here?" he asked the snake.

The snake nodded and Brutus turned and ran toward the barn. Charlie and Scrump scrambled to catch up with him.

"What are we doing?" asked Scrump.

"I saw an old hat in here," said Brutus as he squeezed through the barn door. "If we give it to the snake, she can put her eggs in it."

"That's a good idea!" Charlie said. "Then her eggs will be safe from rolling around and she won't have to lie."

They found the old hat and ran to take it to the snake.

"Oh," said the snake when Brutus told her what it was for. "That will work perfectly. Thank you all so much."

"You're welcome," they replied.

"You might want to try the house," the snake suggested. "Usually, animals that have collars stay closer to the house."

The three friends scampered back up toward the house. They stopped by the back porch where they found a fat orange cat laying on the railing.

"Excuse us," said Charlie, and the cat opened one yellow eye.

"We found this in the garden," Scrump said, pointing to the collar Brutus had carried. "Do you know who lost it?"

The fat orange cat stretched and yawned. "I wondered what happened to that! Thank you for bringing it back."

"You're welcome." said the friends.

The sun started to set.

Scrump, Brutus and Charlie walked back to the barn.

"I had fun today," said Scrump.

"I did, too," said Charlie. "Thanks for letting me play with you after I thought Brutus was being a bully. I will try not to jump to the wrong conclusion again."

"That would be good," said Brutus. "Not every situation is what it first looks like."

"What do you guys want to do tomorrow?" Scrump asked with a mischievous smile.

ABOUT THE AUTHOR

Tif E. Boots wrote her first children's book as a birthday present for her daughter. Many years later it has been shared with her sister, cousins, classmates and now you.

Tif was raised in Marana, Arizona and was working concession stands at county fairs in Arizona and Michigan with her family until she graduated from Marana High School in 2000. She became a mother and correctional officer in 2004. She then moved to Nevada, Missouri with her family where she was blessed with her second daughter and fell into a career of nurse's assistant for Hospice.

Tif and her family relocated to Mulberry, Florida in 2017. In her free time, Tif can usually be found on the water or at amusement parks spending time with family and friends and simply enjoying the life that God has blessed her with.

ABOUT THE ILLUSTRATOR

Syranity Barker is an illustrator who has always had a love for art. She was born in Tucson, Arizona and eventually moved to central Florida where she graduated high school.

Syranity illustrated her love of drawing early in life; her family were great supporters of her passions and always made sure she had a variety of supplies and mediums. While still in high school, her work was entered in numerous art shows. She received the *City Commissioners Choice Award* for a mixed media portrait of her dog and has sold several pieces of her work.

Still fresh out of high school, Syranity works two jobs and illustrates professionally in her spare time. She is currently the in-house illustrator for *ShelteringTree.Earth Publishing* and also promotes herself as a free-lance artist.

Syranity enjoys singing, skating, spending time with her friends and family, and creating her own characters and writing backstories for them.

Syranity aspires to become an art teacher and share her passion for drawing and self-expression with others.

Discussion Guide for Book Clubs or School Classes

1. Why was Scrump running at the start of the book?

_____

_____

_____

_____

2. What hits Brutus in the head?

_____

_____

_____

_____

3. Why is the squirrel throwing acorns?

_____

_____

_____

_____

4. Why do you think the squirrel sees Brutus as a bully?

_____

_____

_____

_____

5. If you were Brutus or Scrump,
   would you still play with Charlie?

_____

_____

_____

_____

6. What does Brutus find in the
   garden?

_____

_____

_____

_____

7. Do the animals keep the collar for themselves? Why or why not?

_____

_____

_____

_____

8. Who is the first animal they ask about the collar?

_____

_____

_____

_____

9. Was the frog helpful in finding the owner of the collar? Why or why not?

_____

_____

_____

_____

10. Why do the friends leave the frog at the pond?

_____

_____

_____

_____

11. Why did they go to the barn? Who did they speak to there?

_____

_____

_____

_____

12. What is the snake doing when the friends find her?

_____

_____

_____

_____

13. Did the snake have a good reason for lying about owning the collar? Why or why not?

_____

_____

_____

_____

14. What was Brutus' solution for the snake's eggs? Was it a good or a bad solution?

_____

_____

_____

_____

15. Who is the true owner of the collar?

16. How do you think the cat lost the collar?

17.What were the differences between Brutus' and the cat's collars?

_____

_____

_____

_____

18.What animals wear collars and why?

_____

_____

_____

_____

19. One of the animals in this story was wrong. Who was it? Why was he wrong?

_____

_____

_____

_____

20. One of the animals in this story lied. Who was it? Why did she lie?

_____

_____

_____

_____

Use the map on the next page.

Mark the path the three friends follow.

Write the page number that goes with each stop along the way.

Draw the animals they meet at each stop.

What do you know about these animals?

Write three details for each one.

_____

_____

_____

_____

SHELTERING TREE
Earth Publishing
ShelteringTreeMedia.com

For more information,
to become one of our authors, translators,
or illustrators,
or to contact the author or illustrator:

ShelteringTreeMedia.com